MR.DIZZY

by Roger Hargreaves

Mr Dizzy was, to be quite honest, not very clever.

If you were to ask Mr Dizzy what was the opposite of black, he'd say, "Er. The opposite of black is . . . er . . . pink!"

He lived in a house on a hill which he'd built himself.

A not very clever house!

One of Mr Dizzy's problems was that he lived in a country where everybody else was terribly clever.

Cleverland!

Even the birds were clever in Cleverland!

Everything and everybody in Cleverland was clever.

You'll never see a worm reading a book anywhere else but Cleverland.

Poor Mr Dizzy. Everything around him was so clever it made his head spin.

One morning Mr Dizzy was out for a walk when he met a pig.

"What's big and grey and has big ears and a trunk?" said the clever pig to Mr Dizzy.

"Er! A mouse?" said Mr Dizzy.

The pig laughed sarcastically at Mr Dizzy, and went off shaking his head.

Then Mr Dizzy met an elephant.

A clever elephant.

"What's small and furry and likes cheese?" the elephant asked cleverly.

"Er. A pig?" replied Mr Dizzy.

The clever elephant laughed down his trunk. "A pig?" he trumpeted. "A pig? You silly man!" And off he went.

Poor Mr Dizzy!

Mr Dizzy decided he didn't want to talk to anybody else that day, so he went for a walk in the wood, where he knew that he wouldn't meet anybody.

He felt very miserable about not being clever, and as he walked along a tear trickled down his cheek.

Poor Mr Dizzy.

Then, in the middle of the wood, he came across a well.

Little did Mr Dizzy know that it was a wishing well.

The day was warm, and so he decided to take a drink of water from the well.

Mr Dizzy drank deeply.

But, he was still unhappy.

"Oh, I wish I could be clever," he sighed.

Little did Mr Dizzy know that, whoever drinks deeply from the water at the wishing well, his wish will come true.

And Mr Dizzy had wished that he could be clever.

And his wish had come true.

He was clever.

But he didn't know it.

Not yet!

On the way home, Mr Dizzy came across the elephant and the pig he had met earlier.

They were telling each other about how they had made Mr Dizzy look silly by asking him a question he couldn't answer.

They were giggling and sniggering about it, when they saw Mr Dizzy approaching from the wood.

"Here he comes again," giggled the clever pig.

"Let's ask him another question," sniggered the clever elephant.

Mr Dizzy came up to them.

"Tell us," said the clever pig, trying to keep a straight face. "What's white and woolly and goes Baaa?"

"Why, a sheep of course," replied Mr Dizzy.

The pig and the elephant were amazed.

To tell the truth, so too was Mr Dizzy.

He suddenly felt very very clever.

It was a not unpleasant feeling.

"Tell us," said the clever elephant. "What has four legs, a tail and goes Woof?"

"How easy," replied Mr Dizzy. "A dog of course!"

The clever pig and the clever elephant couldn't understand how Mr Dizzy had become so clever in one morning.

Mr Dizzy couldn't understand how he had become so clever in one morning.

But we know how he'd become so clever in one morning.

Don't we?

"Now, let me ask you a question," said Mr Dizzy to the pig.

"You?" grunted the pig rudely. "You ask me a question? Don't be ridiculous! There's no question you could ask me that I couldn't answer!"

"Really?" smiled Mr Dizzy. "Well then, can you tell me what's fat and pink and goes Atishoo, Atishoo?"

"What's fat and pink and goes Atishoo, Atishoo?" repeated the pig looking worried. "There's nothing that's fat and pink and goes Atishoo, Atishoo!"

"Nothing, eh?" said Mr Dizzy, and he tickled the pig's nose.

"Atishoo, Atishoo," sneezed the pig.

"The answer is you," said Mr Dizzy. "You're fat and pink and you're going Atishoo, Atishoo!"

The clever pig looked downright, if not downleft, miserable.

Mr Dizzy turned to the elephant.

Who, incidentally, had stopped sniggering.

"Now," said Mr Dizzy. "Let me ask you a question. What's large and grey and goes Dopit, Dopit?"

"What's large and grey and goes Dopit, Dopit?" repeated the elephant looking worried. "There's nothing that's large and grey and goes Dopit, Dopit."

"Oh yes there is," grinned Mr Dizzy. "There certainly is something that's large and grey and goes Dopit, Dopit," and he tied a knot in the clever elephant's trunk.

"Dop it! Dop it!" cried the elephant, who wanted to say, "Stop it! Stop it!" but couldn't talk properly with a knot in his trunk.

Mr Dizzy grinned, and went home.

"I duppose doo dink dat's fuddy," said the elephant.

3 Sixteen Beautiful Fridge Magnets – any 2 for £2.00! inc.P&P

They're very special collector's items!
Simply tick your first and second* choices from the list below
of any 2 characters!

1st Choice

☐ Mr. Happy
☐ Mr. Lazy
☐ Mr. Topsy-Turvy
☐ Mr. Bounce
☐ Mr. Bump
☐ Mr. Small
☐ Mr. Snow
☐ Mr. Wrong

☐ Mr. Daydream
☐ Mr. Tickle
☐ Mr. Greedy
☐ Mr. Funny
☐ Little Miss Giggles
☐ Little Miss Splendid
☐ Little Miss Naughty
☐ Little Miss Sunshine

2nd Choice

☐ Mr. Happy
☐ Mr. Lazy
☐ Mr. Topsy-Turvy
☐ Mr. Bounce
☐ Mr. Bump
☐ Mr. Small
☐ Mr. Snow
☐ Mr. Wrong

☐ Mr. Daydream
☐ Mr. Tickle
☐ Mr. Greedy
☐ Mr. Funny
☐ Little Miss Giggles
☐ Little Miss Splendid
☐ Little Miss Naughty
☐ Little Miss Sunshine

*Only in case your first choice is out of stock.

--- **TO BE COMPLETED BY AN ADULT** ---

To apply for any of these great offers, ask an adult to complete the coupon below and send it with the appropriate payment and tokens, if needed, to MR. MEN OFFERS, PO BOX 7, MANCHESTER M19 2HD

☐ Please send _____ Mr. Men Library case(s) and/or _____ Little Miss Library case(s) at £5.99 each inc P&P
☐ Please send a poster and door hanger as selected overleaf. I enclose six tokens plus a 50p coin for P&P
☐ Please send me _____ pair(s) of Mr. Men/Little Miss fridge magnets, as selected above at £2.00 inc P&P

Fan's Name _____
Address _____
_____ **Postcode** _____
Date of Birth _____
Name of Parent/Guardian _____
Total amount enclosed £ _____
☐ I enclose a cheque/postal order payable to Egmont Books Limited
☐ **Please charge my MasterCard/Visa/Amex/Switch or Delta account** (delete as appropriate)

Card Number

Expiry date ___ / ___   **Signature** _____

CUT ALONG DOTTED LINE AND RETURN THIS WHOLE PAGE